Behind the Willow:
a poetry collection

edited by David Allan Hamilton

DeeBee

www.deebeebooks.com
www.ottawawritingworkshops.com
www.facebook.com/DavidAllanHamilton/

ISBN: 9781896794303

Contents

RHIANNON COBB

morning light from my apartment

Light creeps over the side of the church
Shimmering honey dripping over the stained glass
windows
Drowning the night's misdeeds in soft, sweet day.

park bench

Each year
each season
each day
I remain
your friend
despite time passing
despite all weathering
a person might face
I ask
and will only ever ask
one thing:
Sit with me awhile.

the bookstore

Heavy, creaking wooden door shuts behind you:
The smell of books older than you
The whirr of excited whispering voices
Finally finding Fanon
Tucked behind Beyond Good and Evil
Arms heavy with books
But heart light
And mind clean
A fresh palette.
There is more to learn than can be known
But try anyway
And start here.

the cafe

Lovers in the cafe don't bother me.

With their incessant giggling.
Oozing onto each other,
Molasses
Slurring speech like they have peanut butter stuck to the
roofs of their mouths,
Like their words are honey oozing out of their manic
grins.

Wide, crazed, gazing black pupils
Drugged, drooping eyes.

Grasping hands,
Grazing, squeezing, switching
Touching, always touching,
Like if they aren't they'll slip off the Earth.

Lovers in the cafe don't bother me.

untitled 1

Zooming, zipping through streets
Hugging corners like close friends
Morning air clinging cold to our bare skin

Past cars
Past drivers,
Furious
To see *us:*
Two wheels, one girl
Passing *them*
Still bodies, sputtering engines

They think only of their destination,
We forget ours by the time we arrive.

Behind the Willow

What moves in the shadows, just beyond your eyesight? What creeps just beyond earshot in the black hush of night? You are convinced there is something, but you know you are alone... that there is nothing there... nothing... there.

But you listen for a sign, of the *thing* that is there, that you feel in your spine. In the next room, or waiting on the porch outside. Behind the willow, so delightful in daylight, but in whose shadows something sinister hides. In the piercing silence you will yourself quieter. For your heart to stop pounding, for your staggered breath to cease! Lest they hide the sound of a twig snapping, a board creaking, a sign, any sign, that something is there, something is there.

red

You were blue,
Calling to me.
I dove in deeper,
Cool, cleansing water.

I was white
Quiet.
Clean calm sheets waving in the summer wind,
That made your bed soft when you'd danced through
the day.

You were red
Hunger, burning.
Lipstick that makes you look twice,
Blood dripping from a cut that hurts in just the right
way.

I was white,
Cold.
Muffled voice on a snow banked road,
Looking out the windshield speeding through a blizzard
at midnight.

untitled 3

The world is on fire,
Nobody seems to mind
The mountains burn.
Still we dance
On the cathedral's ashes
And continue on our way
Flames in our wake
Little arsonists

untitled 4

Your name is a comfort of a home that is gone.
But in the dark of night I can't remember hers
And that is comfort enough.

untitled 5

Stranger in a city,
Where nobody knows your name.
You won't be here long enough,
For them to learn it

All the doors are closed to you.
Only with time would they open.
To embrace you,
Let you in.

But you hadn't thought of this.
Your home is far away.
Your train leaves at midnight,
And there are stranger streets to roam.

sunday, 2 a.m.

Thirsty comrades
In arms against curfew and the coming night

Giggling, whispering,
So no one hears our yelling, hysteria

Danny has a curfew but he'll be back out
Through the window of his basement bedroom

We'll still be here, we'll stay all night
The smell of liquor growing on our breath

Pass around the bottle along with the moon
In the dancing, clambering night

Rolling our eyes at the sun as it returns
Hesitantly, after missing the party

Teasing Danny for having to go
To Sunday morning service

Our parents gave up last year
On reeling us home with empty threats

They are far away from us now
Like last week's classes and Monday morning's bell.

DAVID ALLAN HAMILTON

broken skate, circa 1950s.

Whose curled toes slipped into you?
Extra socks, woolen socks, riddled with holes
The crisp February air on the frozen river

Your blade rusted out like the old oil drum behind the
barn
Threadbare laces snap in brittle resistance
To my touch

Cobwebs dust the opening
Gather in the spaces between the boot, the blade,
the forgotten dreams
When the lad was eight

Racing through morning chores
To don the skates before school
Mother waving, doorstep tumbler

Her voice lost in the wintry wind
In the smell of grey ice
The *clack* of frozen rubber on laminated spruce

Father pretends to mend the fence
Steals a glimpse, or two
Was that a smile?

The lad raced across the patchy rink
Pushing hard, lungs aglow
Cheeks in danger of frostbite

The moment captured on Father's camera
Forgotten in a musty scrapbook
The scrapheap of forsaken days

secrets

Still August night, when the ghostly moon creeps over the lake, its obsidian surface wheeples like dark diamond in the gloomy glow of shadow beams. Whispers of a dying breeze ruffles the sleepy leaves and kindles the embers aglow. She sleeps in the tent, spent from the day's adventure, the laughing swim, quiet time in the company of loons, the reading, the wonder of stars, and I with that stone of shame and dismay, slinking toward me in dim recognition. Oh Luna's beauty suffocates and suffocates some more, till I can't breathe, till I can't breathe.

to dine on the grape

1.

A budding musician named Frank
Was told that his playing was rank
He practiced some more
Till he fell on the floor
And wound up with some cash in the bank

2.

A little old woman from Perth
Was known for her gaiety and mirth
One day she did giggle
And her body did jiggle
Till she died and wound up in a hearth

3.

Gerry was one lonely grouse
Because he was missing a spouse
To weigh lay his strife
He searched for a wife
To make a new home in his house

4.

There once was a chemist named Joe
Who had a penchant for Merlot
To dine on the grape
Was his only escape
When the fume hood was ready to blow

a cabin soft

Salamander days of harsh lines
Whispered in dark passages
The muted voice, the crimson voice
Passing of stars and brittle bones
Crack and snap like chalk-face words underfoot
A cabin soft against the water

No magpie moon could match
The pathways rooted in spires
Of fireflies aligned against wisps of
Milky Way jettisoned along the shine
Of candlelight, of candlelight
A cabin soft against the water

Withered lament of better days
Different plays on bitter words
On phrases, squeezed in paragraphs
Sutured into rhymes and patterns that strain
Each word slinks one step closer to its own meaningless
death
A cabin soft against the water
A cabin soft against...

you start with the eyes

You start with the eyes, always the eyes, the eyes that long, that leak, that pierce the dark with their own darkness and scrape the mask from your most private secrets, the grave secrets, the ones that only you and God will ever know, the nowhere lies behind the eyes. Yes, start with the eyes.

Candlelight flickers on empty space surrounding the eyes, adding texture, and colour, the bruised colour of long days and longer nights, the crying colour, the screaming shock of red, of black, of the purple brush on the tongue's palette, signifying nothing, signifying everything.

The mouth is set. You set it there with your filth and hate and gas lighting ways. Pursed and broken, no words come forth, the utterance of the mute, the utterance of the dead, the silent voice that is no more.

You end with the hair, offset, a glint in the candlelight, capturing the flicker like old movies, black and white movies, silent movies, the *flick flick flick* of the flapping strip after the reel runs down and out and spins you into oblivion.

haiku with no title

Endless wintertime
A broken dream disappears
Under the snowfall

KARRIE MOQUIN

a story about a rainy day

We are just outside
you in your fur coat,
me bundled and bleary eyed, throat raw.

You give me the look, accusatory.
I'm not going.
You said nothing about rain,
wet sidewalks. *Puddles!*

I give you the look, eyebrow raised.
You are going.
I'm sick; I've dragged myself
out of bed for this.

Fine then. We do the whole walk.
Around the pond.

Fine then. No shortcuts.
And off we go; you trotting, me hunching.

When we come back you are pleased
with yourself.
As if it were all your idea.

Shaking water off in all directions.
Tail busy, fur coat sticking up
every which way.
Ready for a treat, a game.

As for me;
I saw nondescript shrubs — there, by the pond,
each stark, fragile branch
adorned
with glistening necklaces of glass beads.
And wasn't it something to see!

flying over the west river

If you've ever driven
up
to the crest of the hill and then
down
to the Meadowbank Bridge
as I have

Have you noticed
your spirit
soar ahead and join
the gulls
shining in the cloud-light
as I have?

screen porch in fall

All summer long
    you sheltered us
Now your screens
    are down
You are free

Birds fly joyous through
    your open arms
Leaves whirl on
    your dance floor
Nothing screens
    your ocean view

How wonderful to be a
    screen porch in Fall!

the seagulls

I arrive back home and
  because it's May,

the seagulls have no time
  to bicker on my lawn

Tractors sow the fields!
Lobster boats fish off shore!

A seagull has a busy time of it
  in May

by the shore

I miss the little dog who took offence to saucy waves running frenetically to the shore, with their thousand bubbly feet. How he would pounce and bark and try with all his poodle-might to catch them! I miss this one I hold now too, as she was as a pup. How she would lose herself in the joy and freedom of sand and sea, busy with the chase of the other two, busy with the chase of shorebirds and waves. She is the only one now. She spends her days drowsy, but loathe to be left behind. Content to be carried to the shore. I am equally content to have her small warmth in my lap. The wind dances around us, offering up long remembered scents to her aged nose. Now all at once the wind turns sharply towards us, as if to challenge the setting sun's intention to keep us warm. As if to challenge our own resolve to linger... linger a little longer by the shore.

where new love and grief overlap

Euphoria runs amok
in daylight
laughter bubbles up

Misty shadows of dread
at night
claw at my back

Despite your arms
tight around me,
I wake not knowing
when
there will be
light

RAYMOND AUDET

untitled 1

You're a portrait in blue pastel
under a layer of charcoal

A beautiful spoon of nettles
that I wish I could stop eating

A triumphant call for change
who brandishes hidden knives in the
hidden dark of a throat

A wisteria
drawing me in

You're the one that melted snow
when the sun rose

untitled 2

That black it—
Consumed
some with lead,
Took the glass terrarium.
Corrupted my head,
Defamed my sacrarium.

A mirror—
Awakened that man,
Drain a blue pint from the neck.
In circles they ran,
Algorithm cause a wreck.

Sorry. Sor—
I'm taking it down,
From where the grave-walker slept.
What he'd give to drown,
Under where the moss had crept.

It's packing—

untitled 3

A catacomb crash
Cause pale white bones splintering.
She was in her lane.

untitled 4

And I left him there,
The bottom of the driveway.
A steep hill to climb.

untitled 5

Manic lumination / feigned face
Rolls upstairs to the karman line.
Ocean space suffocate / moon-meet
where no planet orbit

shackle / split / lacerate / drop
Knees clipped (Clip his knees! Clip his knees!)
Locked in monsoon

Lost beneath the sputter.

Float under the trudger

Surface from the gutter

Melt into fine powder

Escape! Impossible!
Forget! Impossible!
Cry Fake! Impossible!
Awake, Impossible!
Amend, Impossible
Hide in a Box Impossible!
Condemn the Impossible!
Foolish Impossible!

Captivation. Captivation. Captivation. Captivation.
Captivation. Captivation. Captivation. Captivation.
Captivation. Captivation. Captivation. Captivation.
Captivation. Captivation. Captivation. Captivation.
Captivation. Captivation. Captivation. Captivation.
Captivation. Captivation. Captivation. Captivation.
Captivation. Captivation. Captivation. Captivation.
Captivation. Captivation. Captivation. Captivation.
Captivation. Captivation. Captivation. Captivation.
Captivation. Captivation. Captivation. Captivation.
Captivation. Captivation. Captivation. Captivation.
Captivation. Captivation. Captivation. Captivation.
Captivation. Captivation. Captivation. Captivation.
Captivation. Captivation. Captivation. Captivation.
Captivation. Captivation. Captivation. Captivation.
Captivation. Captivation. Captivation. Captivation.
Captivation. Captivation. Captivation. Captivation.
Captivation. Captivation. Captivation. Captivation.
Captivation. Captivation. Captivation. Captivation.
Captivation. Captivation. Captivation. Captivation.
Captivation. Captivation. Captivation. Captivation.
Captivation. Captivation. Captivation. Captivation.
Captivation. Captivation. Captivation. Captivation.
Captivation. Captivation. Captivation. Captivation.
Captivation. Captivation. Captivation. Captivation.
Captivation. Captivation. Captivation. Captivation.
Captivation. Captivation. Captivation. Captivation.
Captivation. Captivation. Captivation. Captivation.
Captivation. Captivation. Captivation. Captivation.
Captivation. Captivation. Captivation. Captivation.

untitled 6

The music cut out
And the camera was spinning.
The glint in my eye
Well, it just started twitching

And what do you know
When you live on the roadway
You're so far apart
Still you long for a good day

But when did it happen
How did it go by
You could say I've a longing
But nowhere to fly

Whatever you want
I will follow all orders
If it comes
to it, soon
I will cross all the borders

If you tempt me again
you know just what I'll say
Just a little bit longer now
Just wait another day

You know that I want to,
That I could never look back
I let it all happen
Like a homing attack

When it began, they had already been broken by the
boughs of insanity

untitled 7

Wheat field, blowing wind
Turbine, northward pinned
Sky white, crows had skinned
Scarecrow, never sinned

Patchwork horror, deified
That detached mouth, never lied
Scar-torn fingers, calcified
Metal framework, lost inside

Bleeding carpets
More obscure
Tinted windows
Sad chauffeur

Guarded bunker, asks about
Torn down knee cap, scream and shout
Lacks a conscience, knocked it out
Mad at no one, all my fault

PEARL WILLIAMS

spring

On the cusp of arriving
Welcomed by all
Except winter which must retreat

dawn

Some welcome the new day
Some get ahead of themselves
And are up before dawn

Others pray for an extension of night
Perhaps they retired late
Or perhaps they didn't sleep well
Perhaps they drank too much and were hung over.

Still others know not whether it is night or day
They just lay there ...
silently trying to focus!

the bargain hunters

Time isn't money
For the bargain hunters
The satisfaction is derived simply from the discount
Never mind the price
The time invested may be just as much
To save ten cents on a dollar
or ten dollars on a hundred dollars
For them, the discount brings, sheer, unadulterated
pleasure.

laughter

I laughed out loud this morning
I laughed out loud at noon
Today is laughing-stock day

april

April is a month which brings showers
Much regarded as the true arrival of Spring
Perhaps a little less known,
 it is often regarded as the month of tax terror
So many people are consumed by the fear of not getting
their taxes done on time
Not getting them done accurately, an unexpected large
tax bill
This creates unease for the less than fully organized.
They search through papers
They open previously unopened letters…in search of
that elusive tax receipt.
A low-grade panic sets in if important ones are missing.
And so, it continues.
This fear accompanies the taxpayer everywhere,
 like the ankle bracelet placed on prisoners
so that their whereabouts can be known at all times,
There is no real respite until that day when, the taxpayer
sits down,
Starts, and finally completes that tax return,
whether alone, or with the help of a tax professional.
The feeling on completion is profound relief
It's like walking out of that final exam into bright
sunshine.
Is there a *Tim Hortons* nearby? It's coffee time!

unconvinced

They peddle ideas for a living. Some charge a lot for
their few words.
Others are more generous with their offerings. The
critics set the bar, describing it as "a rent of ability"
Just who do they think they are really. Truly, they're not
that special.
Haven't you had enough of those "talking heads?

They pretend to know so much. But in reality,
if you scratch the surface – they know so little.
I could spend a lifetime exposing them, one after the
other,
and there would still be more of these charlatans, why?

Because we live in a period which is euphemistically
called "the information age".

grief

She was overcome by grief
She was overwhelmed
She did not expect him "to go so soon".

coherently

Coherence is highly regarded
Yet incoherence reigns
Does anyone really care?

the romance of exotica

You have been cooped up
For an extended period
Looking out at a white landscape
Leafless tree branches
People wrapped up in thick coats
Hats and gloves,
Animals huddled inside barns or homes
Can you resist the tug of exotica

The blue-green ocean
The warm summer-like breezes
The pastel coloured buildings
And yes, the scantily clad girls and women

Your spirit is immediately lifted by such sights
Your heart considerably warmed
Full immersion is sought
And frequently achieved

All five senses are performing at a level ten
Faces are all smiles
Hearts are at the ready
And that's usually when it happens
You fall madly in love with everything and everyone in
proximity.

triggered

They started the dialogue
With a gun
And that ended too.

ACKNOWLEDGEMENTS

This collection is made possible by the fine efforts of the writers in the Spring 2019 Poetry Workshop held in Ottawa, Ontario. I am grateful for their enthusiasm and honesty. I would also like to thank Léa Raymond-Marshall for the production of this collection.

David Allan Hamilton
Ottawa, Ontario

If you liked this collection, please leave a review on Goodreads and/or Amazon. Thank you for your support!

www.ingramcontent.com/pod-product-compliance
Lightning Source LLC
Chambersburg PA
CBHW021939170626
46807CB00007B/3196